MOOMIN's

lift-the-flap

Hide and Seek

PUFFIN

Moomintroll and Little My
are playing hide-and-seek.

3 4 5 6 7 8 9 10

Coming, Little My, ready or not!"

Is Little My hiding in the tent?

Is Little My hiding behind the flowers?

Is Little My hiding
in the pond?

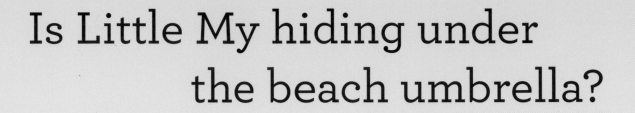

Is Little My hiding under
the beach umbrella?

Is Little My hiding
behind the door?

Is Little My hiding
under the table?

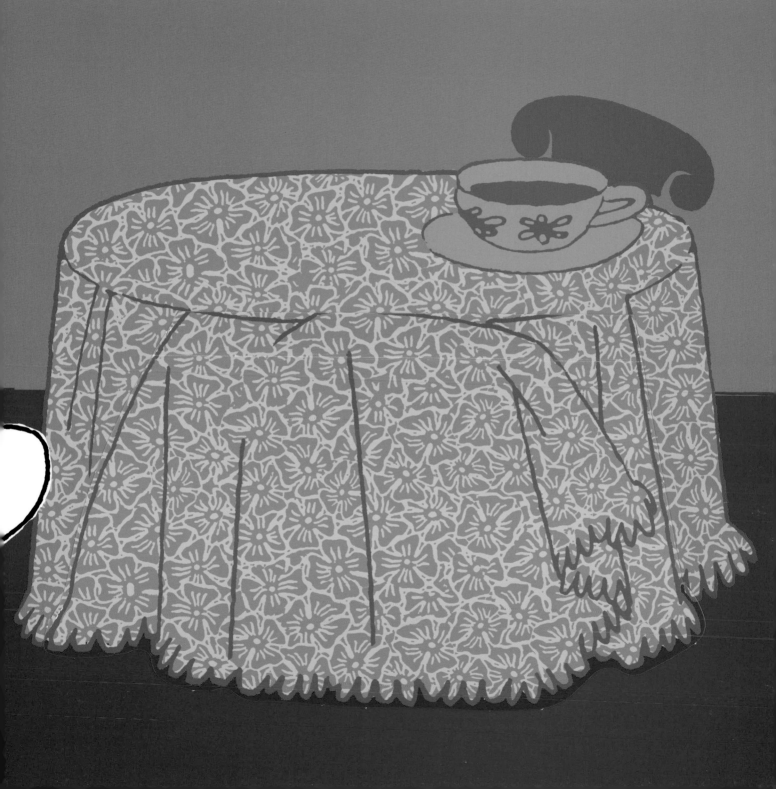

Is Little My hiding behind the newspaper?

"Moominpappa, where,
oh *where*, is Little My?"

"Well, I *have* been keeping something under my hat ..."

"Pee-hoo! I found you Little My. What a clever place to hide!"

"Hee hee hee!"

PUFFIN BOOKS
Published by the Penguin Group: London, New York, Australia,
Canada, India, Ireland, New Zealand and South Africa
Penguin Books Ltd, Registered Offices: 80 Strand, London WC2R 0RL, England

puffinbooks.com

First published 2010
0 0 8
Characters and artwork are the original creation of Tove Jansson
Text and illustrations copyright © Moomin Characters™, 2010
Made and printed in China
ISBN: 978–0–141–32875–1